To Kathryn & Eva

Happy trails

and

God bless America!

Yankee
Doodle
Davey

Travels With Trudy

Trudy Gets Hitched

by Y.D. Davey & T. Ricotta

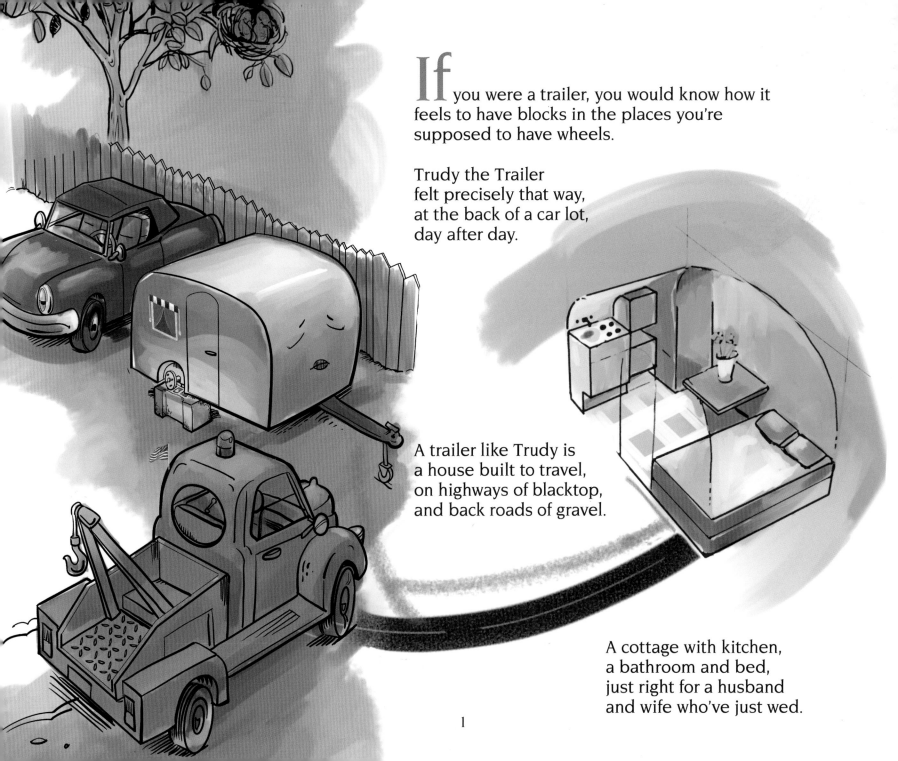

If you were a trailer, you would know how it feels to have blocks in the places you're supposed to have wheels.

Trudy the Trailer
felt precisely that way,
at the back of a car lot,
day after day.

A trailer like Trudy is
a house built to travel,
on highways of blacktop,
and back roads of gravel.

A cottage with kitchen,
a bathroom and bed,
just right for a husband
and wife who've just wed.

1

To travel, two wheels on this home are required,
and a car out in front that's too strong to get tired.

But a car out in front that
would pull and would guide
her, would be of no use:
Trudy's wheels…
were inside her!

Yes, the fellow who
managed the lot, sure enough,
had put them inside her…
with all kinds of stuff!

Clean me out,
put my wheels on,
I'm ready to go…

All I need is a friend
who is ready to tow.

A partner who's
happy through
sunshine or shower;
one who can make many
smiles per hour.

There was one special car that Trudy looked up to.
The car she hoped, someday, she might be hooked up to.

It was Ollie the Auto
she loved and admired;
Ollie the Auto…who
had just been re-tired.

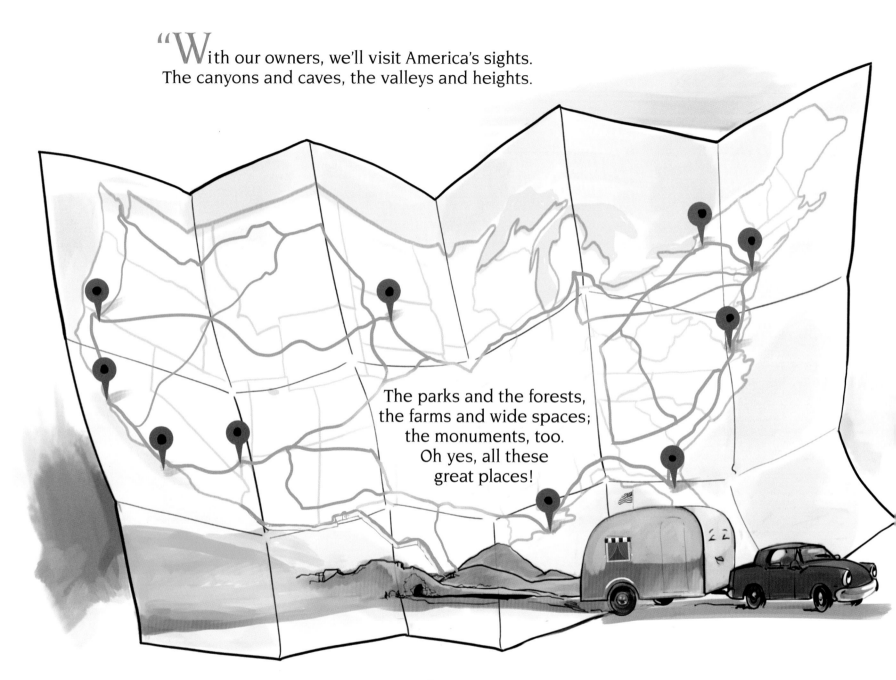

"With our owners, we'll visit America's sights.
The canyons and caves, the valleys and heights.

The parks and the forests,
the farms and wide spaces;
the monuments, too.
Oh yes, all these
great places!

4

San Francisco's a place
we could start with, by golly.
We'll go up and down hills…
with a cable car trolley!

We can camp out at
night in a park
on a ridge.
What a view we
could have of the
Golden Gate Bridge.

5

From there,
we could go,
to see, if you
please,
Giant Sequoias,
the world's
largest trees.

GIANT TREE →

Yosemite Park is one place you can view them.
Some are so big, you can walk or drive through them!

6

Where next, you might ask, of all the great places?
How 'bout Mt. Rushmore, with those four giant faces?

Washington,
Jefferson,
Roosevelt,
and Lincoln.

Did you just catch one of those
presidents winkin'?

7

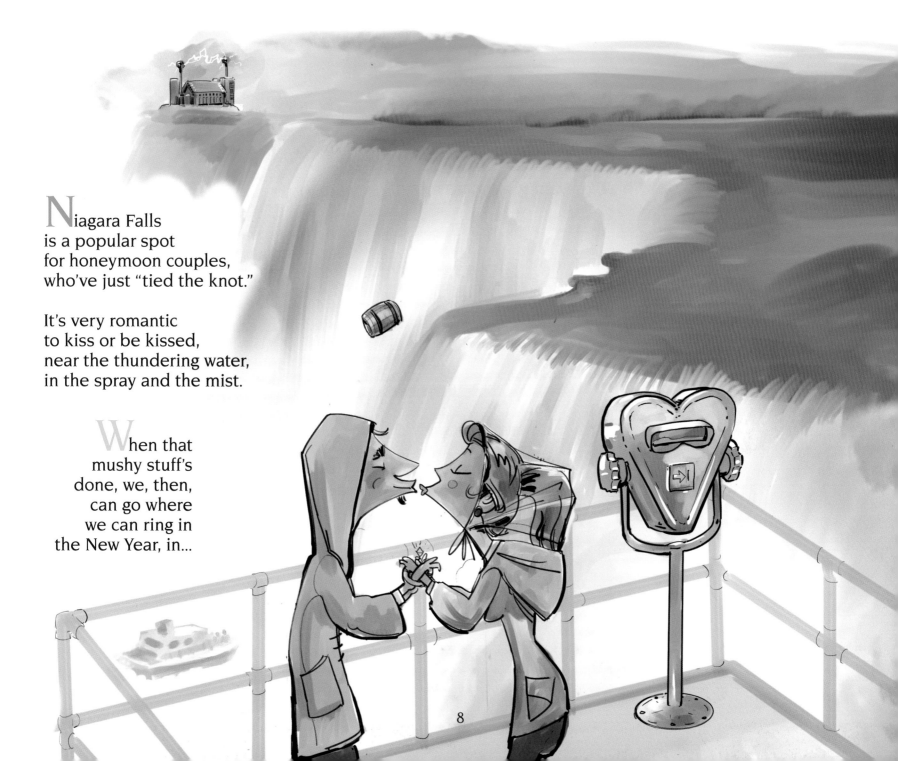

Niagara Falls
is a popular spot
for honeymoon couples,
who've just "tied the knot."

It's very romantic
to kiss or be kissed,
near the thundering water,
in the spray and the mist.

When that
mushy stuff's
done, we, then,
can go where
we can ring in
the New Year, in...

8

New York's
Times Square!

9

We also should visit the famous Bronx Zoo,

then drive past the Empire State Building, too.

10

The one sight to see,
at the top of the list—
The Statue of Liberty.
She cannot be missed!

She stands in the harbor,
three hundred feet tall,
to represent freedom
and justice for all.

Washington, D.C., should be our next stop;
our capital's sights are sure hard to top.

The monuments move you,
no matter your age, but, in spring,
cherry blossoms still take center stage.

If your visit is long,
or your visit is short,
see the Capitol,
White House, and
Supreme Court.

12

Florida's FUN!! There is so much to do.
You can go to the beach and amusement parks, too.

In Daytona, each year,
there's a big stock car race.
In Cape Canaveral,
we blast into space.

When camping in
Everglades National Park,
it's best to stay in,
when it starts getting dark.

From Florida's sunshine, it's not a long trip
to exciting New Orleans, on the old Mississip'.

10 MPH

13

The Mardi Gras party goes on day and night,
with revelry, costumes, and nonstop delight.

But of all the attractions that New Orleans has,
the thing it has most of is New Orleans jazz.

They play it on balconies,
rooftops, and stairs;
it's played in the streets…
and nobody cares!

When we've
heard enough jazz,
we may think it is best
to seek out some quiet
in our country's Southwest.

We'll see cactus, coyotes and cowboys and cattle. Stop in your tracks if you hear a rattle.

We'll see deserts and mountains, one after another, and one wondrous sight that's unlike any other.

15

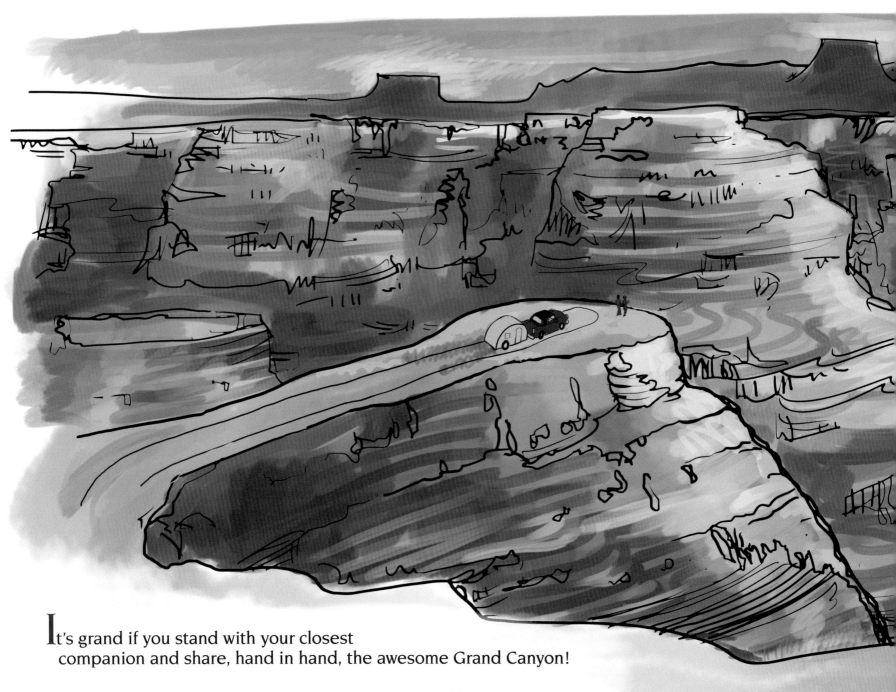

It's grand if you stand with your closest
companion and share, hand in hand, the awesome Grand Canyon!

While we're out in the West,
we might spend a day
at the dam, second biggest,
in the whole USA!

That's a lot of concrete,
but a lot's what you need,
when the job you have forever
is to hold back Lake Mead!

HOOVER DAM

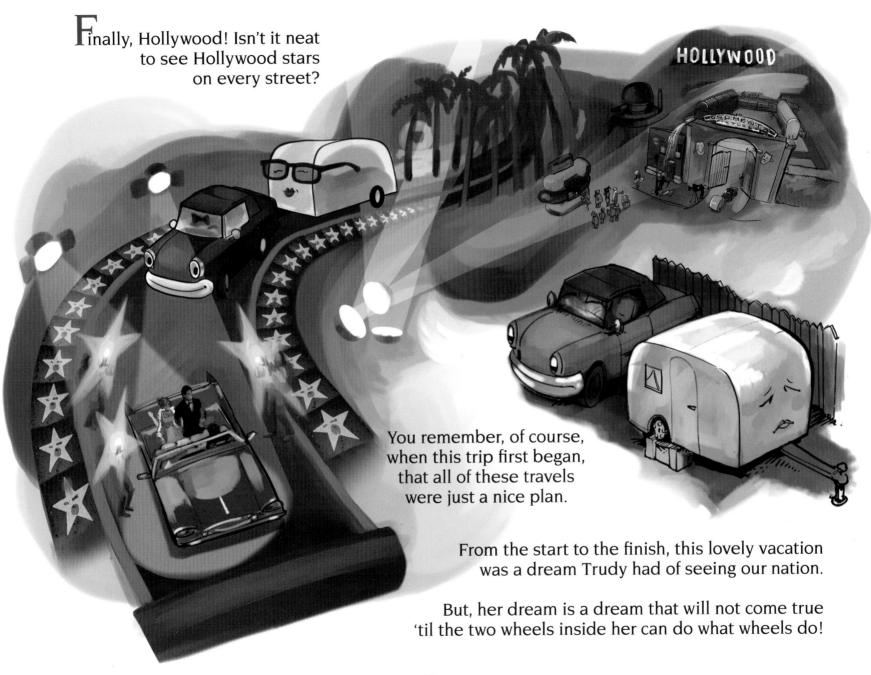

Finally, Hollywood! Isn't it neat
to see Hollywood stars
on every street?

You remember, of course,
when this trip first began,
that all of these travels
were just a nice plan.

From the start to the finish, this lovely vacation
was a dream Trudy had of seeing our nation.

But, her dream is a dream that will not come true
'til the two wheels inside her can do what wheels do!

But wait just a minute, what's happening here?
A husband and wife have the manager's ear.

"Our honeymoon travels will take us quite far. We'll trade our roadster for that trailer and car."

Knowing you're wanted
and feeling you're needed
are two things that trailers
(like people) think can't be exceeded.

So, you can imagine, just how it feels, when a trailer is once again wearing its wheels.
Then, as everyone watched, around the whole lot, Ollie was pulled from his old parking spot.

Dreams can come true, for, now, as you know,
Trudy got hitched to her dreamed-about beau.

And, now, the lot manager said with some flair,

"I pronounce this
fine trailer and auto
...a pair!"

Just Hitched

Just Married!

With Ollie
out front and the
newlyweds in,
it was time for the
rest of their lives
to begin.

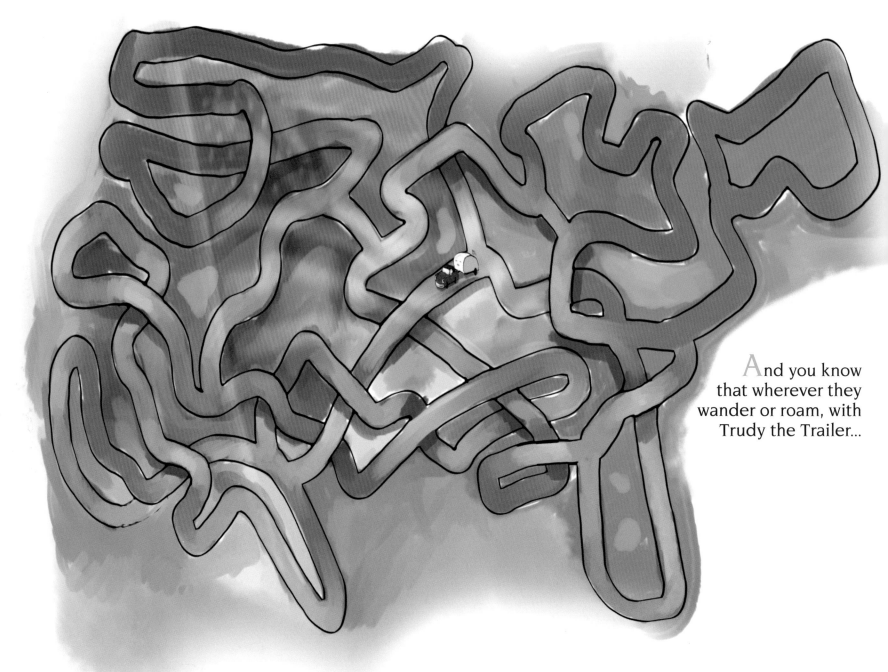

And you know that wherever they wander or roam, with Trudy the Trailer...

they'll always
be home.

Happy Trails.